CRIMINALLY EVIL

CRIMINALLY EVIL

Jason M. Burns

DARBY CREEK
MINNEAPOLIS

Darby Creek
An imprint of Lerner Publishing Group, Inc.
241 First Avenue North
Minneapolis, MN 55401 USA

For reading levels and more information, look up this title at www.lernerbooks.com.

Image credits: zef art/Shutterstock (cover); Rosen Graphic/Shutterstock (texture); idwan kurnia/Shutterstock (font); PERFECT_VECTORS/Shutterstock (font).

Main body text set in Janson Text LT Std.
Typeface provided by Adobe Systems.

Library of Congress Cataloging-in-Publication Data

Names: Burns, Jason M., 1978–author
Title: Criminally evil / Jason M. Burns.
Description: Minneapolis, MN : Darby Creek, [2026] | Series: Demon hunter | Audience term: Teenagers | Audience: Ages 11–18 | Audience: Grades 7–9 | Summary: After a burglar dies during a break-in, high school demon-hunter Damon must face his guilt and fears, and with help from his demon-hunting friends, confront the intruder who returns from the dead for revenge.
Identifiers: LCCN 2025012903 (print) | LCCN 2025012904 (ebook) | ISBN 9798765670668 library binding | ISBN 9798348028190 paperback | ISBN 9798765691915 epub
Subjects: CYAC: Demons—Fiction | Revenge—Fiction | Supernatural—Fiction | Friendship—Fiction | LCGFT: Superhero fiction | Novels
Classification: LCC PZ7.1.B88535 Cr 2025 (print) | LCC PZ7.1.B88535 (ebook)

LC record available at https://lccn.loc.gov/2025012903
LC ebook record available at https://lccn.loc.gov/2025012904

Manufactured in the United States of America
1 – TR – 12/15/25

To Hunter and Eloise—hunt down what makes you happy in life and don't be afraid to face your demons.

1

It's snowing pretty hard right now. I can barely see five feet in front of my face. It doesn't help that I'm pressed belly down on the ground, slowly sinking into the eighteen inches of snow that has already fallen. What a way to spend a day off.

My phone vibrates somewhere in the insulated layers of my snow pants. I bite down on the tips of my glove and rip it off with my teeth. The cold wind stings my fingers. I reach down into my pocket and fish out my phone. I answer the incoming call and hold the phone to my ear. My hand shakes.

"This is not a great time," I whisper.

Madelyn's voice comes out of the receiver, but it's muffled by the knit cap I have stretched over my head. "I need at least ten more minutes, Damon."

I sigh and a tiny plume of freshly fallen flakes tickles my nose. I have to stifle a sneeze. "I don't think I can last another ten minutes. It's *really* mad now."

"Where's Liam?" Madelyn asks.

I shake my head even though she can't see me. Staying active, even with the smallest of motions, keeps my blood from freezing in my veins. At least, that's what I tell myself. This has been the coldest couple of days Salem has experienced in decades. It's not fit for person or beast out here. And yet, here we are.

"I haven't seen him since Frosty tossed him into the foundation of the house that's under construction," I whisper. "I'm on my own out here."

There is a pause. Madelyn doesn't respond at first. I know she's working as fast as she can, but that won't keep me from being packed into a frozen Damon-patty by the demon who is currently set on my imminent demise. I can't even see if the thing is out there. The attack could come at any moment. The snow is just too dense as it falls down. I'm a sitting duck.

"Fine," Madelyn finally responds. "Six minutes."

Before I can negotiate any additional time, the drift I'm hiding behind explodes. It's like someone has dropped a giant sack of flour on top of me. I push myself up on all fours and poke my head out of the snow. The snow demon has found me.

This is probably where I should clarify that my friends and I hunt demons in our spare time. We happened to have a lot of spare time these last few days because school has been canceled all week. First, it was closed because of a frozen pipe, and then, because of the snow, which has been coming down for days. Up here in Massachusetts, they call this kind of storm a nor'easter. Mother Nature has been relentless. Unfortunately, demons don't take snow days.

The demon now staring me down has taken possession of someone's snowman. I'm not sure what kind of demon is inhabiting the thing, but I can confirm that an evil snow sculpture is surprisingly terrifying. Instead of a carrot for a nose, it has two of them sticking out the top of its freshly packed head. They look like horns. Its eyes are two pieces of coal, but they're actually glowing embers that continue to sink deeper into its snowy skull as the coals cause it to melt. And its mouth—the part of the thing that will give me repeating nightmares for the foreseeable future—is a massive, gaping hole with four-inch-long icicles for teeth.

It sneers at me as it glides across the snow in my direction. "I was raised from The Pit to do one thing and one thing alone. Hug!"

So, this might be a bit confusing, but I can clear it up pretty easily. English isn't a first language for most demons. Some can barely speak it at all. This one was probably schooled in English before it was sent up here to see through whatever its mission is. And my guess is that its teacher was a trickster demon. I'm quite familiar with tricksters, but more on that later if I can get out of here in one unfrozen piece.

The point is that the three-tiered

snowman demon is saying "hug," but it definitely means "kill."

"And now I'm going to hug you until you're nothing but a memory," it says as a threatening follow-up.

See what I mean? Last I checked, you can't hug someone out of existence. If you could, my nana would have squeezed the life out of me ages ago.

The demonic snowman advances on me, collecting up more and more snow as the frozen precipitation sticks to it. It grows wider and more imposing. I try to escape, but the snow from the destroyed drift is packed in around my calves and feet. I can't move. I'm stuck.

As I stare down the snowman's grin of sharpened icicle teeth, I'm aware of only one thing . . . six minutes have definitely not passed yet.

The snowman's arms are a pair of spindly tree limbs, brittle but with pointed angles. Each branch ends in an offshoot of smaller twigs that act as fingers. It reaches for me, and the twig fingers uncurl as if growing and stretching out toward the sun.

"You have the honor of being my first hug," it says, and for a second, I convince myself that "hug" is all it wants to do to me. The human brain is an incredible thing. Even its defense mechanisms are a mystery. We can truly persuade ourselves to believe anything if it benefits us in some way. I guess mine just wants to give me a bit of comfort before the horrors I'm about to experience begin.

But deep down, I know I'm not about to be hugged. And I know I can do nothing to stop the thing that is *actually* about to happen to me.

2

Thankfully, there's someone else here who can do something about it.

"Watch me shred this powder, bro!" I hear Liam's familiar voice holler out from behind the demon.

Without any legs to pivot on, the snowman orbits its top two spheres around just in time to watch my BFF coming down on it from above. Liam is riding a plank of wood like it's a snowboard. He drives both the plank and himself into the bewitched snowman. Even with the possession magically holding each frozen flake together, the force is too much for the creature to take. The snowman fractures, crumbling to the ground in piles of clumpy, wet snow.

Liam steps over the piles and reaches down to pluck me out of the compacted snow. He picks me up like I'm a discarded scarf and then places me back down onto my feet. He's strong. Like, really strong. I once watched him juggle a trio of terror bird eggs while walking backward in three feet of sewage. That may not sound impressive, but terror birds are basically the pterodactyls of demons, and their eggs are the size of a garbage can and weigh more than a small car. How is Liam capable of this? Well, he happens to be a trickster demon.

Yes, I know I just said that I both hunt demons and that I'm BFFs with one, but it's true. For starters, Liam is not like other demons. He doesn't want to light the world on fire and roast marshmallows in the flames. He just wants to live out a human existence, though I know for a fact he'd rather do that without homework. Homework is one part of the human world that Liam just can't wrap his trickster brain around.

"It's pretty funny that it kept saying it was going to 'hug' you," he says, chuckling to himself.

See? This is why I'm familiar with the

trickster brand of humor. There's no dad joke in existence that Liam won't laugh at. He even has a joke book from the 1970s that's filled with them.

I reach down and grab one of the carrots that doubled as the demon's horns. I hurl it into the storm out of frustration. It disappears somewhere within the cloud of falling snow. I never hear it land. The howling wind drowns all of the other sounds out because it's whipping through us with an unrelenting fury. I've just realized that I can't feel my toes.

"Where were you?" I bark, annoyed that I almost got murdered by a snowman.

Liam reaches down and snatches up the second carrot. He takes a bite. His open-mouthed chewing only increases my level of annoyance.

"It tossed me pretty far," he says casually. "I landed in that construction site over there. Slapped down hard on a couple of steel bars used to shape the foundation."

Liam lifts his jacket up to reveal three gaping holes in his abdomen. Each wound is about three inches in diameter. None of them bleed, however. That's because Liam's human form is just a suit of skin that he wears to blend in with the rest of the world. His trickster identity is buried deep within the costume, and it takes more than a couple of steel bars to defeat a demon.

"It took me a bit of time to peel myself off of those bars," he goes on to say, finishing off the carrot as he does. "I couldn't get any traction because of the snow."

I instantly feel bad. I know that Liam has my back. He always does. If he could have been out here by my side any sooner, he would have been.

And then a thought that only just recently entered and exited my head returns.

It takes more than a couple of steel bars to defeat a demon.

If that gem is true—which it is—it would take more than a gnarly snowboard trick to defeat a demon, too.

Something in the air shifts. There's an energy to it—like the kind of electricity that a summer thunderstorm can conjure up. The undeveloped neighborhood we're standing in no longer smells pure like newly fallen snow. Instead, it now smells oily and a bit like rotten eggs.

"Get behind me," Liam says as he spits a wad of carrot cud onto the ground.

In front of us, the snow starts to pull itself together, reshaping itself into a humanoid form. It builds and builds, growing at least seven feet tall until it is looming over both of us. A snowy head forms—lizard-like with a protruding snout—and eyes pop to the surface. The eyes are acorns, the pointed caps doubling as pupils. The snow splits and forms a mouth.

"I'll hug you both at the same time," the demon warns.

I hear Liam giggle, but it's sort of in the background. What my ears are locked in on is the sound of whirling propellers, a continuous hum that I recognize well.

A drone descends down from out of the storm. It hovers over the demon.

"The cavalry has arrived," I say. "Meet Screech."

The demon looks up at Screech, our drone backup that Madelyn is always equipping with new tools to help us on our hunts. She named it after her favorite breed of owl. She fancies herself a bit of a birder. I'm not sure what kind of upgrades she has given Screech this time. I just know that it took at least six minutes to get the job done.

The demon laughs. "Am I supposed to be scared of a little . . ."

The demon's words are cut short as a stream of fire erupts from a nozzle attached to Screech's underside. The flames melt the demon down, taking with it all of the snow in the general vicinity. All that remains is a patch of soggy, singed earth.

"Did you turn Screech into a flamethrower?" I ask in a state of shock.

Madelyn's voice comes through the drone. "Actually, it's more of a holy oil flamethrower. I wanted to make sure the demon wouldn't be able to regenerate again. That's why I needed more time to get it equipped. I didn't want the holy oil to drain out on the flight over from your house."

We use a lot of weapons in our war with demons, but anything deemed holy—basically, those things blessed by a religious figure—tend to be our go-to ammunition. That's because they're the most effective.

Liam slaps his hands together, causing me to startle. "Well, that settles it then. Can we get out of the cold now? I'm having a hankering for some hot chocolate."

Screech tilts to the right and then points itself in the opposite direction. It flies off. "I'll put the water on," I hear Madelyn's voice say as the drone disappears into the storm.

It takes at least fifteen minutes for me to be able to feel my hands and feet again. My fingers come back online a little quicker than my toes because of the warm mug of hot chocolate I have them wrapped around. Even sitting next to the vent in the living room where the heat pumps out is not nearly as cozy as it sounds. I feel chilled down to my bones.

Liam, Madelyn, and I are all back at my house. The three of us have been using my house as our base of operations for the last few days because my dad has been on a constant stream of work shifts given all of the problems that the winter weather has been causing.

He's a police officer here in Salem. During times like these with the frigid temperatures we're having, there are always people in need of help. And helping others is what Dad does best.

"I still say we should have done something," Liam says, tossing his body back on the recliner.

He's no longer looking at us, but instead, is facing the ceiling. His long, muscular physique hangs over the chair. He's twice as big as most of the kids in our high school. Coach Davis has tried unsuccessfully to recruit him to the football team countless times. You have to admire his persistence.

Madelyn glances between both of us, trying to grab hold of the thread in the conversation. Her pale skin is nearly as white as the newly fallen snow. She was born with albinism, which means her body lacks the ability to make melanin, the pigment that gives skin, hair, and eyes their color. The genetic condition makes it very dangerous for Madelyn to be out in sunlight without protection. It's why her parents moved her here from Texas not that long ago. They wanted to get her as far away from the equator as possible.

"Done something about what?" she asks.

From where I'm sitting by the vent, I can only see the soles of Liam's feet thrown back on the recliner. The heel of the sock on his left foot has a big hole in it. Just looking at the exposed skin reminds me of the iciness outside.

"We saw some dude breaking into a house a few blocks away," Liam responds.

I lean forward, hovering my face over the vent as the boiler kicks on. The gush of warm air is like an island breeze. "We don't know that for certain. He could have locked himself out of the house and lost his house key in the snow or something."

Liam scoffs. "Yeah, 'cause a lot of homeowners wear ski masks when they're climbing through their own window."

"It's negative ten degrees outside," I say. "It's even colder if you calculate in the windchill. He'd be a fool if he didn't have a ski mask on. Besides, it doesn't matter anyway. I texted my dad about it. They'll check it out."

"Wait," Madelyn says, pausing, "you texted your dad? Won't he be curious why you were out walking around in this weather?"

I wave off the worry. "I told him that Liam and I got brave and wanted to try sledding McCluskey Hill while the powder was still fresh."

Liam snickers to himself. "Brave? Pff. If we were brave, we would've confronted the guy."

"Don't give me that," I say, kicking the recliner that Liam is sprawled out in. "This is not something new to what we do, Liam. When we started hunting, we agreed that we would only focus on demons."

That's not entirely true. Sure, we primarily hunt demons, but we've faced plenty of other unexpected baddies before.

There was that one time we had to drive a group of mischievous pukwudgies out of the forest by Puck Bridge Lake. Pukwudgies aren't demons, but you could argue that they're demon-adjacent.

Still, anything to do with humans seems off-limits. I don't need to be stepping on my dad's toes, and he certainly doesn't need to know what the three of us are up to when he's not around.

The thing is, people don't have any real clue what the world is actually like. No one really believes in demons because they can't see them. Demons have a tendency to disguise themselves whenever they're on vacation in our neck of the woods.

I bet if we held a survey of everyone in Salem, more people would believe in a reindeer with a glowing red nose than a demonic entity with glowing red eyes.

That goes for my dad, too. He sees the world in black and white. To him, there are good people and bad people.

Me, I see the world in shades of gray. I recognize that there are good and bad people all around us. But I also see—*physically* see—that there are the occasional demons thrown into the mix. And guess what? They're not all bad.

Liam, for one. If I were to just paint everyone in the same two colors that my dad sees the world in, I'd have never had the chance to call Liam my friend.

As long as I can remember, I've been able to see auras. An aura is like a fingerprint for the soul. Everyone's got one, and everybody's looks different. No two are exactly the same, even those that belong to identical twins.

After my mom realized I had this gift of what she called a "second sight," she helped me better understand it. She fancied herself a spiritual seeker, which meant she studied a lot of practices meant to achieve inner peace. She had read about people who could see auras and taught me that seeing an aura was not as important as reading one.

I can learn so much about a person by reading their aura. I can tell what kind of pasta they prefer (Madelyn's aura screams pappardelle, a flat, waving ribbon of a noodle), if they like sauce on top, or even if they want it served al dente. Which, let's be honest, anyone who doesn't want it al dente has their priorities all out of whack.

But I can also tell when someone is not a some*one* at all. A demon's aura looks completely different than a human's.

For example, Madelyn's is almost entirely filled with color and shimmer. Her aura looks like mica, a kind of rock that Mom and I used to collect on our hikes throughout the White Mountains of New Hampshire.

As for Liam, his aura is more like a twisting knot of darkness and despair. His does have an important detail that stands out from other demons, though. His has the faintest hint of color—an inner glow that I call his aura's heart. It's the piece of his aura that told me he was inherently good. That's not a normal feature in the auras of other demons.

"Let me ask you something, Damon," Liam says, interrupting my train of thought.

I don't say anything, so Liam moves on to just asking his question.

"If it were *your* house that dude was breaking into, would you have a different opinion on if we should have done something or not?"

I look over at Liam in the chair. He is staring up at me from his horizontal position. He's got a big grin on his face—the kind that curls slightly upward with "you know I'm right" corners.

"Again, you're just assuming that guy was

breaking into that house," I say, though I know I'm quickly losing the argument.

Liam reaches down and grabs hold of the recliner's handle. He pushes it forward and shifts his weight along with it. His body goes from horizontal to sitting up straight.

"Okay, let me rephrase," he says. "If I *thought* someone *might* be breaking into your house, would you want me to do something about it or just walk away and go have a big cup of hot chocolate?"

"I don't have time to keep arguing about this," I say, though, the truth is, I have plenty of time. "I've got to work on my essay for Miss Noe, and my dad should be home from his latest shift soon."

"Who does schoolwork on a snow day?" he asks, but it's more of a rhetorical question.

Madelyn stands and starts to wrap her body in her winter gear. "I did all of mine this morning before we even started the hunt."

Liam's face scrunches up in disgust. "Gross." He slips his feet into his snow boots by the door and turns to Madelyn. "Come on,

I'll walk you home. If that guy in the ski mask really was trouble, I don't want you out in this storm alone with him."

My body twitches, and my eyes open.

It takes me a moment to realize how exactly I got here . . . and where "here" even is.

I'm lying in my bed with an open English textbook spread out over my chest. There's a small stream of drool running down my chin and pooling up at the base of my neck. I'm pretty sure there's a highlighter jammed deep into my right armpit.

I sat down on my bed earlier to do some reading for my essay. I must have dozed off.

I turn my head to look out the window. It's dark outside. The sun sets at around four thirty in the afternoon this time of year. It could be any time after that. How long have I been asleep?

I hear a jarring bang coming from somewhere down the hall. The sound causes my body to instinctively sit upright. The English book bounces off my mattress and falls to the floor. I hear another bang. Someone—or some*thing*—is in my house.

There is a very good chance that what I just heard is a direct result of my dad now being home. There's also a chance that it belongs to something else that isn't supposed to be here. Here's the thing: you tend to make more than a few enemies when you're out hunting demons as a side hustle. I'm always a little on edge about a vindictive one showing up at my house.

There was also that guy at the house earlier today. Liam thinks he was a burglar. What if that's what I'm hearing now, just like Liam suggested could happen?

I dig the highlighter out of my armpit and quietly climb out of bed. I reach for the bottle of water on my nightstand. It's not actually meant for drinking. The bottle is filled with holy water, making it a weapon. I keep it there, hidden in plain sight from my dad, for a situation just like this.

I creep to my doorway and pause. I listen

intently. There is some kind of jumbling noise like metal clanging against metal. I unscrew the cap on the bottle and slowly lean out through the doorway to peer down the hall.

At the end of the hallway, I spot my dad crouched on one knee by the front door. He's rummaging through an old toolbox.

I lower the bottle, screw the cap back on, and return it to my nightstand. Now that my heart has stopped beating out of my chest, I turn and walk down the hall. My dad hears the creaking of my steps on the floorboards and turns to acknowledge me.

"Sorry if I woke you," he says.

My dad is still wearing his Salem PD uniform. He's a big, muscular guy, a fact that is always more obvious to me when he's dressed in his blues. At home, he usually opts for a baggy sweatshirt, which tends to hide the fact that he's in much better shape than most dads I know. How he keeps fit when he is constantly snacking on pork rinds is beyond me.

"No, it's fine," I say, stopping a few feet from the door. "I must have fallen asleep.

It's good that I'm up now, though. I've got homework to finish."

My dad nods and turns his attention back to the door. I notice a dead bolt lock—the pieces still waiting to be assembled—spread out on the floor by his knee.

"What are you doing?" I ask.

My dad responds but keeps his focus on his current DIY job. "Just installing a new lock. Can never be too safe, right?"

Normally I'd say sure, but our front door already has *three* dead bolts, two more than anyone else I know.

My dad has always been a cautious guy, but that need to shield us from danger skyrocketed to unsustainable levels after what happened to my mom.

She was an incredible singer and had an awesome career in music before she had me. A few years ago, she got an offer to go on tour singing backup for one of the biggest pop stars in the world. She was going to say no, but I convinced her to go. She made it all the way to São Paulo, Brazil, with the rest of the band.

But then she disappeared from her hotel room. No one—including Dad and me—ever saw or heard from her again. After that, Dad got super protective. He barely let me out of his sight for months after her disappearance.

I really thought we had moved past all the extra caution.

"But, Dad . . ."

He holds up his hand, stopping me from finishing my thought. "Before you say anything, this has nothing to do with the past. There's a burglar running around Salem. I'm just adding another deterrent because you'll be here mostly by yourself until this storm lets up."

I start connecting the dots in my mind. The lock. The burglar. The guy in the ski mask that Liam and I saw on our walk home.

"So that thing I texted you about, that was him?"

My dad nods. "Seems so. It has all of the same calling cards of his work. With the snow, he's getting more brazen. It's giving him cover."

"Is he dangerous?" I ask.

My dad stops what he's doing and hesitates

to give a response. The pause tells me more than his words could.

I alter my question. "He didn't hurt anyone at that house, did he?"

My dad stands and turns to face me. "There isn't anything you and Liam could have done. You did the right thing by texting me about it. Anything else would have ended up with you two getting hurt, or worse."

I wish that were true, but it's not. Liam could have made easy work of that guy, and I kept him from intervening. I am responsible for whatever happened there.

"How bad was it?" I ask.

"He got the jump on the man who lived there," he says. "The homeowner got a pretty bad gash on his head—nasty concussion—but the doctors say he should recover fully. Either way, I'm headed back out to catch the guy after I finish this up. We're all out in full force until we can get him off the streets. Now, can you hand me that Phillips screwdriver?"

I kneel down and dig the tool out of the box and hand it to my dad. I don't say anything as I reflect on the situation. My dad says I'm not to blame for what happened to the homeowner, which I understand. But he doesn't know the whole truth, and I'm also not completely innocent, either. If someone just stands by and watches a crime happen, aren't they still somewhat responsible?

My dad takes the screwdriver from me but lets his hand linger on my own. "Remember what I said. It's not your fault."

5

I'm sitting at my desk trying to come up with a conclusion for my English essay that will pack the right punch. I've written down a few ideas already, but none of them are quite right. I'm supposed to be making an argument in the essay, but everything I write seems more like I'm surrendering to the opposing view.

It's late—nearly midnight—but I'm not tired. I'm afraid that unexpected nap has done me in for the night. My sleep schedule is going to be all thrown off. Thankfully, school has already been canceled again for tomorrow, so hopefully, I can get back into a normal rhythm. That's assuming that we don't have another hug-loving snowman wandering out there in this never-ending storm.

My dad made sure I locked all *four* dead bolts when he left. I put the new key on my key ring and it's now official—I have more keys than our school janitor, Mr. Pepin. Maybe we can have a jingle contest whenever school opens back up.

My earlier nap isn't the only thing keeping me up, though. I haven't been able to shake the guilt of not doing anything about the burglary Liam and I saw. I haven't mentioned it to Liam yet. I was going to text him, but I hesitated. I guess I just don't want to hear an "I told you so" right now.

We battle demons on a weekly basis, for crying out loud. Demons are *definitely* worse than human burglars. Why wouldn't I let Liam do anything about the burglar? Why didn't I do something myself?

The air in my bedroom changes, like my own personal jet stream just rolled in from up north. The hairs on my arms stand on end. My lips pucker as a bitter sourness swirls all around me.

I know these sensations well. I'm about to have a visitor.

Boo-en is a paralysis demon. I woke up

one night months ago with him sitting on my chest, siphoning off my energy. It's how that breed of demon feeds. Boo-en, however, was taken aback to see that I wasn't surprised to see him. We struck up a conversation, and, as it turned out, we had a lot in common. We both like to read, and we both don't care for demons all that much. Boo-en always felt a kinship with humans, but that puts him in a weird place down in The Pit where demons live.

After that night, we entered into a gentleman's agreement. I'd let him keep feeding on my energy every night if he agreed to read from the books I'd leave out for him. I had heard somewhere that the human brain still absorbs knowledge while sleeping. So, I figured that I might as well make the most of my REM time. Boo-en eats while reading nonfiction books to me, and I wake up knowing things I didn't know when I went to sleep. I'd call that a win-win.

Tonight is an in-depth breakdown of the Second Battle of Bull Run from the American

Civil War. I checked it out of the library before the storm hit.

But even if I hadn't napped for half of the afternoon, Boo-en would still be early. Why is he here now?

There is an inaudible *pop*, *pop*, *POP* of electricity in the center of my room as a portal appears. Boo-en drops down out of the portal and lands on my plush carpet. He speaks before I can say anything.

"Damon must hide! Damon not safe!"

I lean back in my desk chair. It squeaks beneath the shifting of my weight. "What are you talking about? I'm fine."

Boo-en, who looks like a cross between a prehistoric weasel and a modern-day llama, paces excitedly back and forth on his hind legs. He's frantic and moving in a herky-jerky way, like an excited rooster waiting for its brain to catch up with its body. If Boo-en had feathers, they'd be ruffled.

"Damon hide under Damon's bed!" he shout-whispers. The words come out like a gasp of air.

Confused, I stand but stay anchored in place by my desk. "I'm not going under my bed. I don't even know what you're talking about, Boo-en. You sound completely unhinged, which is saying something because you usually don't make a lot of sense as it is."

Boo-en leaps off the floor and grabs the collar of my shirt. He pulls me in close to him—so close that his acidic breath causes my eyes to water—and he speaks slowly and plainly. He is as serious as I have ever seen him.

"Boo-en trying to tell Damon that Damon not alone! Man is in Damon's house!"

The hairs on the back of my neck flicker to attention.

"If there's anyone in my house, I'm not hiding," I say. "I'm going to get him the heck out of here."

Boo-en shakes his head emphatically. "Man is dangerous. Man will hurt Damon."

I feel myself take offense to Boo-en's warning. I've defeated demons, some of them as strong as gods. I can handle a common human thief.

"Maybe I'll hurt him," I say, my hands clenching into fists.

Boo-en lashes out and knocks his tiny llama fist against my forehead. He's trying to get my attention. "Now Damon sound unhinged. Damon not invincible . . . and man have weapon."

I hadn't considered that.

"What kind of weapon?" I ask.

Boo-en's expression suddenly becomes very somber. He seems to be unfamiliar with the emotion that he's experiencing. His inner demon wants to expel the sensation, but his body is already invested in it. "One that could really, really hurt Damon."

I'm actually moved by Boo-en's concern for my well-being. If my body wasn't currently jacked up on adrenaline, I might have actually told him so. Instead, I start to formulate a plan.

"You're right," I tell Boo-en. "I'm not invincible, but you can make me pretty close to it."

Boo-en looks at me like I have three

heads, which is actually kind of funny given that where he's from, three heads aren't that uncommon.

"Possess me," I say.

Boo-en is about to tell me no when we both hear something shatter somewhere in the house. If I had to guess, the broken thing is a lamp. The noise seems to have come from the living room.

"Damon not hide under Damon's bed?" he asks, looking for confirmation.

I stand my ground. I don't answer the question because the fact that I'm still standing in the middle of my bedroom is all the response he needs.

Boo-en sighs and then turns into an opaque vapor that still somehow maintains his physical form. The cloud swirls around itself, becoming a miniature tornado before dispersing in multiple directions and entering my body through my nostrils and ears. All of my senses go haywire, as if they're recalling everything they've ever cataloged about the world. I can smell my mom's perfume. I can taste a jar of pureed sweet potatoes I ate as a baby. I can see the very first aura I ever set my eyes upon.

And then everything goes dark like I've closed my eyes. The thing is, my eyes are wide open.

Boo-en is now in control. Like an IT expert granting someone access to a database they have been locked out of, Boo-en brings me back into the cockpit, though now I'm in the copilot's chair. Boo-en is in charge of my body's actions, but I can see, hear, taste, and smell everything again.

Boo-en moves forward. He uses my hand to reach out and grab the doorknob. He opens the door and a gush of cold air hits us. Somewhere in the house, a window or door is open.

We step out into the hallway. Boo-en's not even trying to stay quiet. We've moved beyond stealth mode. As we reach the end of the hallway, Boo-en turns us into the living room. The window behind the couch has been shattered and the metal screen is bent on the floor. So much for dead bolts.

Everything is dark, but the moon is reflecting off the snow outside and illuminating some of the nooks and crannies of the room. Boo-en scans the space, stopping at a lamp that has been knocked to the floor. The ceramic base has been shattered, but somehow the light bulb is still in one piece.

Boo-en keeps scanning, reaching the far corner of the living room with our shared set of eyes. There, backed into the wall of shadows, is the burglar. A ski mask covers most of his face, but the eye holes reveal that one of his eyes—the left one, to be exact—is mostly white and riddled with scar tissue. He can't possibly be able to see out of that eye.

"Don't move a muscle," the burglar orders, his voice muffled by the ski mask. "If you do, I'll stick you like a juice box."

Boo-en lowers my head. In the burglar's hand, which he has partially concealed behind his thigh, is a large hunting knife. He turns the blade slightly to the side. The moonlight coming in through the window glints off the reflective surface of the blade. It makes it look even more ominous than it already is.

"Damon not be doing any of that," Boo-en says through my mouth. What a strange experience it is to hear someone else's voice inside your own head.

The burglar cocks his head to the side, confused by what he's hearing. "What's wrong with your voice, kid?"

Boo-en steps toward the burglar. The burglar raises the knife in response. While slumped into the passenger seat of my own mind, I study the burglar's aura. It's fully human, but there are telltale signs of a life lived for selfish means. While most of his aura is made up of bursts of green, squiggly lines of static interrupt the color, muting the full potential of who the burglar could be.

"I ain't kidding," he says, his hand shaking a little. "I won't think twice about breaking your mom's heart if you come any closer."

Boo-en inhales a big breath into my lungs. I can feel his anger—anger at the burglar's mention of my mom—and it's taking all of

Boo-en's willpower not to attack the man.

"Damon has no mom because men like you make world a cruel place," Boo-en says.

The burglar has no idea what to make of this late-night run-in. Surely, he thought he'd be in and out of my house with his score in no time. I was a twist in his plan that he did not anticipate. He side-eyes the window he entered through, no doubt wondering how fast he can get back through it without cutting himself on the broken glass.

My paralysis demon pal is prepared to help test that theory for him.

Boo-en reaches up with my hands and spreads my jaws open. Before the burglar can even see it, I can *feel* the tentacle slithering its way up my throat and over my tongue. The flavor of caramelized ash assaults my taste buds as the tentacle pushes out through my mouth, scraping against my teeth. The burglar's eyes—one as white as the pearly white flesh of the tentacle itself—go wide in terror.

"Now go!" Boo-en's voice shouts, but it doesn't come from my mouth. Instead, it just hangs over the room like a ghostly recording with the volume set on high.

The burglar drops the knife and sprints toward the broken window. He leaps headfirst over the couch, diving through the window like a dog that has mastered an agility course. The shards of glass cut into fabric and flesh, but the burglar clears the obstacle. Boo-en and I run to the window just in time to see the terrified man sprint from my front yard into the street . . .

. . . and right into the path of an oncoming snowplow.

7

I'm standing in the bathroom brushing my teeth in front of the mirror. No matter how many times I do it or how much toothpaste I use, I can't get the taste of the tentacle out of my mouth. I'm going to need a lifetime supply of mints.

"That's like the sixth time you've brushed your teeth since everyone left," my dad says as he walks by the bathroom, stopping in the open doorway.

Obviously, I can't tell him why I'm scrubbing my mouth like it's a bathtub covered in soap scum, so I keep my response vague.

"I guess I just have a bad taste in my mouth," I say after rinsing.

My dad leans against the doorjamb and inspects me with his eyes. Having a cop for a dad, I'm used to visual examinations, but this one is different. He doesn't suspect something. He's trying to figure out how to *heal* something.

"It's not your fault," he eventually says.

I shake my toothbrush off, smacking it against the side of the sink, and then return it to its place in the medicine cabinet. "I know."

He ignores my acknowledgment and continues on with his prepared parental pep talk. "You must have scared him when you came out of your room. He took off because he didn't want to get caught. He didn't want to go to jail. I'm thankful that was his play, to bail on the situation, instead of doing something with the knife he brought with him."

I nod, moving past my dad and walking back to my bedroom. I see the time on my clock as I enter. Three in the morning. After everything that happened, the house became a busy crime scene. All of Dad's coworkers showed up with him—everyone worried that I was hurt—and then the detectives and medical examiner appeared shortly after that. The plow driver was pretty shaken up, too. Dad had me make him a cup of tea. He was an absolute wreck. I think he thought he'd be charged with murder or something. Even though obviously it wasn't his fault either.

Dad follows me into my bedroom. "Do you have any questions that you'd like to ask me? I've been through this kind of stuff before. I have felt what you're feeling."

I sit down on the edge of my bed. I stare down at the floor, examining the carpet as if there's something there even though I know there's not.

"Who was he?" I ask.

My dad looks surprised. "Would that help you—to know that?"

I nod.

"Okay. Well, his name was Evan Wisdom. He wasn't from Salem. He was just using our community as a piggy bank that he could steal from. He'd been hitting it up for two weeks now. We found his car a few blocks over. Footprints in the snow led right to our living room window. He must have cased our house before he decided to hit it. He knew where he was going."

I absorb what he's telling me, but I still want to know more. When you're partly responsible for someone's death, it feels necessary to know as much about the person that you had a hand in . . . hugging.

"What was wrong with his eye?" I ask.

The question has been haunting my mind since I looked into that eye for the very first time.

Again, my dad seems surprised. "I'm not so sure talking about all this other stuff is such a good idea, Damon. There's such a thing as too much information, you know? It's just going to pick at the scab that's growing on your open wound. And believe me, it's an ope—"

I look away from the carpet and lock eyes with my dad. "I need to."

"Need to what?"

"Talk about it," I say. "I need to make some sense of it all."

My dad stares at me for what feels like an eternity. He eventually nods, agreeing to answer my question even if he doesn't agree with the reasoning.

"The eye was from a previous fight he had," he says, releasing the information as if he's reading it from a press release. "He got in a scuffle with someone and . . . well, you saw the results. He couldn't see out of his left eye at all. Detective Hutch thinks he didn't even see the plow coming. He was spooked and just took off, not even taking the time to look with his good eye when he stepped out into the street."

I take in the information. I know I'm not to blame for what happened to Evan, but it's hard not to shoulder some of the responsibility anyway. I'd like to think that he wouldn't have used the knife on me—that we could have resolved things differently—but I don't know that. The entire ordeal could have ended with me dead instead of him. I can't even imagine how Dad would have handled losing me after already having lost Mom.

If only Evan hadn't broken into our house in the first place.

"Speak of the devil," my dad states.

I whip my head around to face him. Any

mention of a devil or demon tends to get my attention. "What?" I ask, the pitch of my voice rising.

My dad holds up his cell phone. "It's Detective Hutch calling. Put a quick pause on our talk?"

I nod as Dad answers the call.

"What's up, Hutch?" Dad pauses. I can hear Detective Hutch's booming voice coming out of the phone with an added layer of bass thanks to the tiny speaker. "No. I'm still here at home. What?!" Dad's face flushes. His dark skin, filled with deep lines caused by the stress of his job, softens. He looks almost childlike. "That's not possible. He must have an accomplice. Yeah, I know. I'll be there in ten minutes."

My dad ends the call with Detective Hutch and then looks up at me, his pre-call personality completely changed.

"I've got to head out."

"Is everything okay?" I ask.

He points at me. His expression is stern, but his aura suggests that he is more like a scared little boy who is afraid to go to bed without a night-light. He's just trying to keep it hidden from me. "Lock the door and don't answer it for anyone. And no matter what you do—don't leave this house!"

8

I run to the living room and look out through the remaining window as my dad backs the cruiser out of the driveway. As he passes in front of the house, I duck behind the temporary cardboard that was hung up to cover the broken windowpane. I peek back around the cardboard and watch until the police car disappears out of sight.

What my dad doesn't know is that Madelyn installed a police scanner on my phone. As long as I'm tuned into the right channel, I can hear everything my dad and his fellow officers are saying to each other over their radios. It's not illegal to listen in on a police scanner, but it's not exactly honest, either. Mostly because I haven't been honest about it with my dad. If he ever finds it on my phone, he'll interrogate me until I confess to the reason for having it. A reason I'm not ready to give him.

Still, I haven't seen him look that shaken since the day we found out Mom was missing. Whatever Detective Hutch told him over the phone, it shook my dad right to his core. And I need to find out what that thing is.

I pull out my phone and press my finger to the police scanner icon I keep hidden in a folder. The app takes a few seconds to load, but when it does, there is already back-and-forth chatter going on between the various members of local law enforcement.

"Affirmative," a young female officer states. "I'm here now with Stashwick. We can confirm the doctor's assessment of the scene. He isn't on the property. At least not anywhere that Stashwick and I can see."

A second officer chimes in. This one is male but high-pitched, like a set of vocal cords trapped inside of a helium balloon. "There is no *he*. Not anymore. It's just a body."

"I understand," she says back, "but that doesn't change the fact that the body isn't here.

The morgue is officially one corpse shy."

Officer Helium sighs. At first, I mistake it for a squeak, but then I realize what it is. Irritation. "Am I the only one who is going to point out that dead guys don't just get up out of the freezer and walk out of the morgue on their own?"

Uh-oh. That doesn't sound good. Like, at all. Unlike Officer Helium, I actually do know quite a bit about dead guys walking around on their own. Too much, actually, and it's never a positive thing for anyone involved.

"You all need to remember what you're saying and where you're saying it." I recognize this voice well. It's my dad's. "These channels are not private. Just the facts are all we need to be sharing, and the fact is, we have a missing body, not a missing person."

So it's true. Evan Wisdom has gone missing. But how? Boo-en and I witnessed what happened to him. Boo-en even tried to help Evan after he was hit by the plow. Boo-en locked my consciousness out of the experience, and I went into the black again for a while. But

I know that he did what he could to help bring Evan back, even though it wasn't possible. Evan had already left his body.

So, where exactly did his body go?

"This is dispatch," a new voice announces over the radio. "Hate to interrupt, but we just got a breaking and entering call through 911. It sure sounds like the usual style our guy has been using. Can someone head over to Towne Street and respond to the call?"

The young woman officer is back. "That's not far from Stashwick and me. We're pulling out of the morgue now, so we'll head in that direction."

Dispatch fires back almost immediately. "Standby, gang. Got another B&E call coming in right now. Same M.O., only . . . this one is across town."

The radios are silent as the officers await more information.

"This is weird," dispatch continues. "We've got another one on top of that. This third one is coming in from a completely different area of town, too. It's over at . . . what the . . ."

“What is it, dispatch?” my dad asks over the radio.

Dispatch’s voice comes back, this time a lot less confident. In fact, it sounds downright shaky. “The lines are lighting up. There are breaking and entering calls coming in from all over Salem. I’ve never seen anything quite like this before.”

“What in the world is happening?” my dad mutters to himself, not realizing that his radio is picking up his self-reflection.

If I could respond to my dad, I would. Demonic activity is what’s happening, and it’s the most brazen kind I’ve ever heard. It sounds like the town is under attack. Someone has to stop Evan before somebody gets hurt.

“Damon is up so late,” I hear a voice say from behind me. The voice speaks in a similar cadence as Boo-en, but the tone sounds nothing like his.

I whip around and face the darkness of the living room. There, in the corner, is Evan. He is standing in the same shadows as he was the last time he was in my house. The only thing different is that this time he isn't alive.

"Damon must be so tired. Let Evan put you to sleep."

Although I can't see his face through the darkness, I can still see Evan's aura, and it's not his own anymore. The bursts of green are gone. The squiggly lines, too. There is a pure black filter draped over his aura like a shroud. The uppermost layer of the filter wriggles with artificial life. The movement resembles an endless sea of skittering insects. It makes my skin crawl.

Evan's body is no longer his to control.

"I know you're not him," I say, trying to nonchalantly dial Liam's number on my phone as my eyes remain fixed on the corner of the room. If I can wake Liam up and he answers, he could at least hear what's happening. He could come over and help. "So, who are you?"

An appendage like an artery lashes out from the darkness. It soars through the air like a dragon in flight and wraps around my phone. The artery snatches the device out of my hand. I'm unable to finish dialing Liam in time. My phone disappears into the shadows as the artery delivers it to its owner.

"That's where you're wrong, Damon," Evan says. I can hear him twist and bend my phone in half, snapping it into two pieces. At least I don't have to worry about my dad finding the police scanner app anymore. "I am Evan—just new and improved. Thanks to you."

He steps out of the corner and into the light. Although physically he is still in the same body, Evan looks nothing like he did the last time he was standing in my living room. Contorted and coiled at odd angles, his limbs have been heavily damaged by the snowplow's impact. There is a large gash across his leg, which was presumably carved into him by the blade of the plow. The wound oozes not with blood, but with maggots. They fall from the cut and hit the floor, writhing at his feet. Evan's scarred-over eye is no longer white. Instead, it glows red like a car's brake lights.

Whatever he is, Evan is no longer a man.

"After you showed me a glimpse of what was possible in this world, I embraced the change with open eyes and open arms," he says. "Sure, I was dead, but that didn't mean I couldn't make a difference. It didn't mean I couldn't still *be* somebody."

I back away, aware that Evan isn't here to finish robbing my house. He's here to finish me.

He stops walking forward, sensing that I could bolt at any minute. He wants to at least finish his story before he attacks me. "I met someone after my heart stopped beating, and it wasn't the driver who plowed into me, though, make no mistake, I'll be visiting with him just as soon as I'm done with you. No, this stranger had an interesting proposition."

I swallow hard. I know where this story is going. "You made a deal."

Evan smiles. His glowing eye twinkles like a set of holiday lights wrapped around a pine tree. "And what a deal it was! Eternal, everlasting life, and in exchange, all I have to do is kill you. Not a bad offer considering that

I would have done that for free anyway. It's all I've been able to think about since you chased me into the path of that plow."

"I didn't chase you," I say, angry at the accusation. "And I certainly didn't put you here in the first place. You chose to break into this house. You made the choice to break into all of those houses. And you ran into the street without bothering to look both ways."

Evan shrugs as he takes another step toward me. His gait is awkward, as if the lower portion of his body could detach and fall to the floor at any moment. The bones beneath his skin crack like tree limbs caught in a hurricane.

"So, what you're saying is, I've made my bed—or grave, as it were—and that I should lie in it?" he asks.

I try to back away further, but Evan flinches. It's a predatory motion that suggests that if I try to escape, he'll be on me in a heartbeat.

Speaking of heartbeat, mine is racing. I can feel it echoing in my eardrums.

"I'm saying you should stop blaming others for everything that has gone wrong. I'm sorry for what happened to you—I am—but you're not a victim. Your choices and actions brought you to this place."

A smile stretches across Evan's face. Most of his teeth are missing. I'm not sure if this is how his mouth has always looked or if his teeth were knocked out when he was struck by the plow.

"So wise for being so young," he says, though I don't take it as a compliment. "It's a shame I have to stop the oxygen flowing to that big brain of yours, but you've made yourself some pretty powerful enemies, including my new benefactor. I think you know him quite well. He's even managed to conjure up some fake robberies all around town so that we can have this private moment to ourselves."

I glance toward the hallway. If I can just make it to my room . . .

"A moment that will be your last!"

I spring away on the balls of my feet before Evan finishes his threat. He's laughing, which is how I know he's pursuing me. I don't look back, but I can hear his coldhearted cackling getting closer as I sprint down the hallway toward my bedroom.

I reach the open doorway and dive inside. I hit the plush carpet with my right shoulder and force myself to roll forward, knocking into my nightstand. Without looking behind me, I reach up and grab the bottle of holy water. I frantically unscrew the cap, spin around, and point the opening of the bottle out in front of me. I squeeze.

A spout of water gushes from the bottle. It hits Evan right in his glowing red eye as he's diving toward me. The demon-tainted flesh sizzles like a freshly cracked egg on a hot griddle. He falls to the carpet and howls, clutching at his face in agony. I quickly scramble up to my feet so that I'm standing over him. I hold the bottle of holy water—still half-filled—above his face. The action is an ultimatum.

"Get out of my house!" I demand.

Evan surges upward, levitating like a falling body in reverse. He knocks the bottle out of my hand. The remaining holy water spills out onto the floor as I collapse back onto my bed.

Evan lowers his hands from his face. His crimson eye is gone. Deep within the darkness of the cavity left behind, I can see another eye looking back out upon the world like a hologram. This eye belongs to whoever is controlling him.

Without saying a word, the levitating Evan flips himself over in the air so that his belly is now facing the floor. He snarls, showing off his toothless muzzle, and accelerates in my direction. I sense the returning *pop*, *pop*, *POP* of Boo-en's arrival as one of his portals opens up in front of me. It's just in time to swallow Evan whole.

10

It's morning. I'm sitting on the floor of the living room, huddled beneath a big quilt that once belonged to my mom. She would use it to snuggle up on cold winter weekends as she watched marathons of house-flipping shows. It still smells like her. At least that's what I've convinced myself. I'm not even cold, but having it wrapped around me makes me feel safe.

Or as safe as I *can* feel after everything that has happened.

Dad has called and checked in a couple of times. He's still out, roaming the streets of Salem. The entire department is on full alert. The many calls that came in about break-ins all turned out to be false alarms—essentially prank calls. But they're still missing a body from the morgue as well as a lot of answers.

My dad's not giving me many details. He thinks he's keeping me safe by not sharing a lot of information. What he couldn't possibly be aware of is that I know more about the case than he does.

"Where did you send him?" Liam asks, once again stretched out on the recliner like a lazy cat. He has a pancake rolled up like a burrito and is shoving it into his mouth.

Boo-en is seated on the couch. I'm too traumatized by last night's events to worry about how the couch is going to smell now that my personal paralysis demon has made himself at home on it. Yellow flakes fall down from his dry skin and cover the surface of the upholstery. I'll have to vacuum it before Dad gets home.

"Boo-en not sure," he says. His tongue stretches out from his mouth and twists upward. He sticks the tip of his tongue into his own ear to clean the passageway out. "Boo-en not have time to think. After Boo-en get Liam and Madelyn, Boo-en come back to find man jumping at Damon. Boo-en react.

Make portal willy-nilly. Boo-en don't think man is far."

Madelyn steps up to my side and kneels down next to me. She places her hand on my shoulder. "Are you okay, Damon?"

I jolt upward, tossing the quilt to the floor. I unconsciously swat Madelyn's hand aside, which I instantly feel bad about. She recoils away from me.

"No, I'm not okay! I just lived through an actual nightmare! A medley of man and demon just attacked me in my own house! If it wasn't for the bottle of holy water I keep by my bed, I'd be toast!"

"Don't worry," Liam says, testing the recliner to see if it goes back any further. It doesn't. "I would have brought you back."

Madelyn raises an eyebrow. "Wait. You can do that?"

Liam sits partially upright, swallows the last of his pancake, and shrugs.

He can't do that.

I sigh and flop back down to the floor. "Evan is going to come back for me. Offing me is part of the deal he made. He has to see it through. He won't quit until I'm dead."

"Let him come," Liam says. "Your dad already agreed that I could sleep over tonight. I'll happily make this dude regret showing his face again."

I glare at Liam. "And what if he decides to come tomorrow night? Or the next? I'll be living in fear until he shows up again."

Madelyn turns to Boo-en. "Could you find out what demon he made a deal with, Boo-en? That kind of information could really help us."

Boo-en considers the question and then reels his tongue in, slurping down whatever it was he dug out of his ear canal. "Boo-en will inquire. Boo-en thinks possession type used is unique. Demon responsible doesn't possess like how Boo-en does."

"I could see the demon's eye," I say as I reach out and grab hold of the quilt. I wrap it back around my shoulders. "It was there—sort of—inside Evan's head."

"If I had a dime for every time we had an empty eye socket make an appearance,

I'd be one rich trickster," Liam says, the words flowing out of him like stream-of-consciousness vomit. "One rich . . . *richster*." He chuckles to himself.

I ignore the pun. "And Evan said that I knew the demon he was working with. Other than you two, I don't *actually* know any demons. It's not like we get chummy with them before we send them back to The Pit."

"That's not entirely true," Liam says. "Remember that one time we played pickleball with those two imp brothers? They weren't all that bad. We even shared an ice cream with them."

"We still sent them back to The Pit," I say.

Liam waves his finger. "Well now, that's not entirely true either. If I remember correctly, we asked them to go back, and they did. That's not sending."

I sigh, frustrated by Liam's recent need to dissect my sentences like he's working on a project in one of our anatomy labs.

Madelyn, always assertive when it comes to deciding on a course of action, takes charge of the room. Between my numbness, Liam's passivity, and Boo-en's . . . well, Boo-en-ness, we absolutely need her to step up.

"Okay," she begins, "here's what's going to happen. Boo-en, you're going to head back to The Pit and start asking around about who might be pulling Evan's strings. I'm going to hit the books and see if I can find anything out about this kind of remote possession. There has to be something written about it in the lore."

"And us?" Liam asks, his eyes closed and his face at rest in a peaceful expression. He's moments away from falling asleep.

Madelyn glances between Liam and me, letting us know that we're going to be a package deal for the rest of the way. "You two are going to booby-trap the house from top to bottom."

I look up at Madelyn from beneath the comfort of my quilt. "We're going to do what?"

"You're going to set traps for Evan. If he comes back tonight, which we expect him to, you need to be ready. You need to make this place a house of horrors for any demon who decides to enter."

Liam shoots upright, returning the recliner to its regular position. "Hey! I'm a demon, and I'm going to be here!"

Madelyn smiles. "Then you better be careful where you doze off later."

I'm really not at all excited about having to turn my home—my family's home, which my mom helped to make feel so special—into some kind of demon snare. This is where I live. This is where I sleep. This is where I feel safe.

Or at least, I used to feel safe here.

Why am I so rattled? I've battled demons as large as dragons. Sure, they were invisible to the naked eye and required me to wear a special pair of glasses from The Pit, but that didn't make them any less real! The point is, this should be nothing for me.

So why isn't it nothing?

11

Liam and I are in the basement of my house. Although it's late in the day, it's still somewhat light outside. We're currently rigging up small tarps of salt above each of the basement windows. If Evan pokes his head through one of them, the trap will trigger and the salt will come down on top of him. It won't send him back to The Pit, but the salt should weaken him. Demons can't come in contact with it without suffering through some serious physical pain—even the common table salt variety.

Liam tends to think with his appetite instead of his common sense, though. He'll eat anything if it tastes good, though that usually ends with him clutching his stomach and complaining about having a bellyache. It's like having a friend who is allergic to gluten but who eats bread with every meal. He just can't be stopped.

Once we get the tarps in place, it's my job to pour the salt in. Liam stands back by the basement stairs to avoid getting any of it on him.

"You were right," I say, climbing up onto the step stool.

"Of course I was," Liam responds immediately. "Wait. What was I right about?"

I reach up above the trap, my knuckles scraping along the exposed pink insulation that is wedged into the cracks of the open ceiling. I start to pour the salt into the tarp. It sounds like skittering insects as the crystals hit the tarp and spread outward.

"About the burglary," I continue. "We should have done something. We should have stopped it from happening. If we had, all of this could have been avoided."

Liam sits down on the bottom of the staircase. He scuffs the soles of his shoes across the rough cement floor. "Meh. You can't control where life goes. You can only deal with whatever comes your way. If it wasn't Evan, it would have been something or someone else."

I finish filling the first trap and climb down from the step stool. I drag the stool across the basement and position it beneath the second window. I climb back up, careful to keep my balance.

"Still, if we're going to do good, we can't just turn away when we see something bad happening," I explain, filling the second tarp with salt. "If we had acted, at the very least, the homeowner wouldn't have gotten hurt."

"How do you know that?" Liam asks.

I keep pouring. The canister of salt is almost empty. I hope my dad isn't planning on making his famous force fries anytime soon. That's what he calls his hand-cut french fries, so named because everyone in the police force loves them so much.

"Because we would have stopped it from happening," I say.

"Pfft!" Liam blurts out. "Not true. Not even close to being true. Evan could have been going *back* into the house to take more. He may have already knocked the homeowner on the head when we saw him. Everything that dude has done is on him and no one else. And you can take that from a demon who chose not to live like one."

I finish emptying the canister of salt into the tarp and then climb down from the stool. I think about what Liam said. I keep partly blaming myself for everything that has happened—to me, to the homeowner, to Evan himself. I think I've kind of accepted this demonic vendetta that has been leveled against me. It's almost like it's punishment for what I've done. Punishment for the hand I had in all that's gone wrong since I chose to look the other way.

"Maybe you're right," I say, though the way I say it isn't all that convincing.

"I'm always right," Liam responds with a smile. "I thought we already established that?"

Though I hate to admit it, he has definitely been right about this. All of it. We should have intervened when we saw Evan breaking into the house. I would have absolutely wanted someone to do the same for my family if it were my house. It's like I've been fighting myself throughout this whole situation. I haven't been able to come to terms with what was always the truth, even though it was right there in front of me. I guess I was too stubborn to admit any of it.

If that's the case, why am I still too stubborn to admit it out loud now?

"Can Damon come out and play?" I hear Evan's voice ask from somewhere outside. It's like the high-pitched screech of a bird of prey. In fact, Evan's voice sounds an awful lot like an angry terror bird watching its eggs get stolen.

Liam shoots to his feet and pulls down on the chain connected to the basement light. There is a click, and the bulb dims. The basement goes dark.

"I promise to make it quick and painless if you don't make me work for it," Evan continues.

Liam motions over to me, whispering as he does. "Your phone. Hand it over."

I managed to transfer my service plan over to my old phone after Evan snapped my newest one in half. I hand it over to Liam. We rigged up the entire house with traps just like Madelyn told us to, including swapping out the knob on the front door with an iron model. Demons hate iron.

Liam clicks on the doorbell camera app, and after a few extended seconds of loading (it was my old phone for a reason), we're able to see Evan standing outside on the stoop of my house. He leans in and peers into the lens of the doorbell camera with his empty socket. Even through the pixelated image on the cracked phone screen, I can see the demon's eye hidden beneath. I can feel its judgment.

"Are you watching me right now?" Evan asks, smiling for the camera. "You are, aren't you? Well, that's a crying shame because that means you're making me work for this. I guess slow and painful it is!"

Evan reaches for the doorknob. As soon as he touches it, a fire ignites in his palm. Evan screams like a wild animal as the fire spreads up his arm. He turns away from the door and plunges his entire upper body into a bank of snow. The fire is extinguished, but the one inside of him grows unruly. He looks enraged as he turns back to the door and glares into the doorbell camera's lens.

"So very slow and so very painful," he promises.

12

Liam and I are static, standing completely still in the dark. Evan is no longer visible on the cracked phone screen, which means he's on the move. He will find another way into the house. There are windows all over and at least two other doors.

"What do we do?" I ask quietly.

Liam tosses me my phone and studies the basement, looking for anything that he can use as a weapon. He settles on the top portion of our artificial Christmas tree, which he holds in his hands like a baseball bat.

"We bring the fight to him," he says, fishing a forgotten ornament out of the dense branches of the tree and tossing it on top of a box labeled "Holiday Decorations."

Evan's feet suddenly appear at the basement window to my left.

"Get behind the washing machine and stay there," Liam whispers.

I do what Liam says, taking cover behind the metal monstrosity that is older than both my dad and me combined. He refuses to get a new one because according to him, "this one works perfectly fine," even though the repairman is out every few months to take a look at it. Last time, we were told that they don't even make the parts to fix it anymore.

Liam ducks behind the boiler, backing himself against the foundation of the house. He holds the tree with the top down by his side. I peer out from behind the washing machine and watch as Evan kneels down to inspect the basement window.

He scrutinizes the darkness and smiles. Content with his latest entry point, he balls his hand up into a fist and smashes it against the pane of glass. The windowpane falls from its frame and smashes onto the basement floor.

"Okay," Evan says from outside the open window. "If Damon can't come out and play, I guess I'll have to come inside. We'll just have to find some way to pass the time in there. What do you think we should do together, Damon?"

From behind the washing machine, I watch Evan bend down and stick his head through the open basement window. He pushes himself in further, and the crown of his head puts pressure on the nearly invisible fishing line, which triggers the trap. The tarp flops down from above and salt crystals pour down onto Evan. His throat releases a bloodcurdling sound—like an animal that has its paw caught in a bear trap—and he retreats back through the window.

I look over at Liam. He holds up his index finger, signaling for me to remain where I am.

"I am going to fillet you like a fish," Evan says as he dives in through the basement window like a missile. He sails into the room past the fallen piles of salt to a clear section of the cement floor. He plants his feet and rises, smirking as he does.

Evan looks around into the surrounding darkness, wheezing through the melted remains of his nose. The salt has dissolved his sniffer, along with a good chunk of his face. Small tufts of hair stick up from patches of skull bone like little islands of trees.

"Where are you, you monster?" he asks.

Liam flippantly steps out from the shadow of the boiler with his arms stretched out at his sides. The tip of the tree scrapes along the floor. Liam is inviting a fight.

"I'm right here, handsome," he declares. "After all, you're looking for a monster. You found one."

Evan looks at Liam and dismisses him almost immediately. He's come for one thing and one thing only . . . me.

"What's wrong, afraid to take part in a fair fight?" Liam asks.

"Not afraid," Evan responds with indifference. "Just not interested."

Liam raises the tree and draws it back like a sword. "Well, you're getting one whether you want it or not!" He soars through the air in Evan's direction, prepared to bring the tree down on him.

As he continues to look around the

basement, Evan reaches up and catches Liam's wrist. The entire action is done in such an unemotional way that it comes off as almost an afterthought.

Evan casually twists his own hand upside down, forcing Liam's arm to turn awkwardly in an unnatural position. He drops the artificial tree and has to crouch down to move with the twisting motion so his arm isn't torn off at the elbow.

Evan glances down to look at Liam.

"Everything you throw at me will fail," he tells Liam. Liam's face contorts in anguish as Evan continues to twist his arm against the elbow joint. "I know how you fight better than anyone."

Liam looks up at Evan and stares into the empty socket that once housed an eye. My best friend's face, normally comfortable and confident, falls into an uncharacteristic expression of defeat.

"No," he says, slinking further toward the basement floor. "Run, Damon. RUN!"

I leap out from my hiding spot and sprint

up the stairs, skipping every other one.

"Yes, run, little mouse," Evan's voice sings in a lullaby as I escape from the basement. "The hunt is on!"

13

I slam the basement door closed behind me and quickly set the trap that Liam and I rigged above the door earlier in the day. When Evan opens it, a satchel of iron nails will fall down from above, just like the salt in the basement. If I'm lucky, he'll catch fire like he did when he touched the iron doorknob.

What did Liam see in Evan's face? What kind of creature is so intimidating that it could fill a trickster demon with such fear? I've never seen my friend respond like that before, even when we faced impossible situations with insurmountable odds. He's always the "glass half full" guy. So what was it that drained his glass and left it shattered?

I back away from the basement door. I keep marching aimlessly in reverse to put as much space between myself and the basement as possible. My heart races, making it feel like I'm halfway through a marathon I didn't train for at all, even though I've only managed to make it as far as the front entryway. My back runs into the front door, the many dead bolts keeping it latched into place. What good are they against whatever Evan has become? What good is anything?

I listen closely for any sounds that may be coming from the basement. I don't hear any fighting. I don't hear any screaming. I don't even hear Liam rifling off any one-liners, a favorite pastime of his whenever he is wrestling with a baddie.

I don't hear anything.

BANG BANG BANG

The pounding at the front door causes my heart to leap out of my chest. I fall forward, collapsing onto the floor of our entryway.

"Damon, it's me," Madelyn's voice calls out from the other side of the door. "I have to talk to you."

I crawl over to the door and press my face against it. I can feel the cold from the outside trying to get in—trying to choke out the warmth just like Evan wants to choke the life out of me. Suddenly, everything feels hopeless.

"Quiet," I whisper into the door, my request sounding like a panicked plea. I'm desperate to convince myself that Evan has stopped looking for me—that perhaps he crawled back out the window he dived in through. But if he hasn't, I don't want to call any more attention to myself. Even though I know there is only a basement door separating Evan and me, it's the only thing keeping me safe. "He's here. He's come for me."

I can hear Madelyn pressing herself closer to the outside of the door. Her words vibrate through the wood.

"That's what I'm trying to tell you, Damon," she explains, still speaking loudly. Too loudly for my frayed nerves to handle. "There is no 'he.' Boo-en asked around. He learned that there is no demon in charge of Evan. There never was."

"No," I say through gritted teeth. "I saw his aura. I saw that he was a demon."

The doorknob twists and turns, but the door doesn't open. "You only saw what you wanted to see, Damon—what you needed to see."

From below me, I hear footsteps ascending the basement staircase. My heart thumps with each stomp of Evan's feet. He is getting closer.

"He's coming," I cry out, dragging myself to my feet. "Get out of here, Madelyn. Save yourself while you still can."

Madelyn starts to pound on the door again. "No, Damon. Let me in. You don't understand."

I turn and press my mouth as close to the front door as possible. "I do understand, Madelyn. I have this coming. It's all my fault, and now I have to pay for it."

The basement door bursts off its hinges, flying into the kitchen wall and splitting down the middle. The force of the supernatural blast rips my trap of iron nails from its housing and sends them crashing to the floor. They scatter across the tiles, some disappearing underneath the refrigerator and stove.

Evan emerges from the basement, his face

now nothing more than bone. There is no sign of Liam.

"Damon is here," he says. "Now, what do you say we finish this so I can get on with my new life?"

14

I sprint away from the front door, fleeing in the direction of the bathroom. Liam and I had set up our biggest trap in there, so I know that it offers my last and only hope. I close my eyes and will my body forward. I have to pass Evan, nearly losing my footing on some of the fallen nails, but somehow, I manage to avoid him grabbing hold of me.

Either that, or he's toying with me.

I make it to the bathroom and open my eyes just as I leap through the air and land in the bathtub that we had previously filled with holy water. Desperate times called for desperate measures, and we had to rely on a prerecorded blessing that we found on the internet to turn the whole batch into a last-minute holy haven. I have no idea if it will even work, but it's better than standing out in the open.

Outside in the cold of the storm, Madelyn is still pounding on the front door. "Only you can stop this, Damon," she yells. "Only you can stop Evan."

I stand in the tub of holy water, waiting for Evan to appear. I hear his footsteps moving across the kitchen tiles. He kicks some of the nails, which whirl about like toy tops. He's whistling now. It's nearly inaudible so I can't recognize the song itself, but I can tell the tone and what it's meant to convey. Joy.

He's taking his time with me. He's enjoying it.

Evan saunters into the open doorway of the bathroom, still whistling his tune. In the bright light of the vanity, his physical appearance is almost too much to handle. I stare, but it's only because I can't look away. I'm frozen in fear.

"You did this to me," he says, recognizing how shocked I am by his appearance. He steps forward into the bathroom. His pulverized hip crunches like a bag of potato chips.

I shake my head. "No, I didn't," I say,

kneeling down so that more of my body is submerged in the holy water. "I didn't do anything."

Evan smiles. One of his last remaining teeth falls from his mouth and clangs off the toilet, plopping down into the bowl. "You don't believe that."

He's right. I don't. I've tried to not blame myself for everything that has happened, but this is my fault. We wouldn't be here if I had just acted in the first place. Nobody would have gotten hurt.

There is banging at the rectangular bathroom window.

"Don't you see, Damon?" Madelyn calls out from the other side of the glass. "It's you! You've summoned Evan to get revenge against *yourself*! You've weaponized your own guilt! You are the one possessing him!"

I hear Madelyn's words, but I don't understand them. It doesn't make any sense. I'm not doing this. I can't be.

"Now, why don't you climb out of that tub so I can give you what you deserve," Evan says.

I look beyond Evan's disfigured face and stare into the empty eye socket. Just like before, when I focus on the darkness within, I can see another eye looking out on the world that doesn't belong there. Only this time, I recognize the eye. It's light brown with flecks of green scattered over it like sprinkles on a cookie.

It's my eye!

"The only way this will stop is if you forgive yourself!" Madelyn hollers.

I glance over Evan's shoulder and look into the bathroom mirror. There, in the reflection, I see the same eye that is buried deep inside Evan's empty socket.

"Come on, Damon," Evan says, "you know this is what you have coming. I wouldn't be back here if you didn't. Stop prolonging the inevitable!"

I try to ignore the terrible sight in front of me. I try to block out the voice. I close my eyes and focus on my breathing, tracking each inhale and exhale. I go somewhere in my mind—a place somewhere deep in my subconscious—and search for forgiveness.

I've said it wasn't my fault. Both out loud and to myself, but I've never meant it. I never *really* let myself off the hook.

That's because I'm to blame.

"Yes, you are," Evan whispers.

With my eyes closed, though, I recognize something in the darkness. Although I know it's just my mind showing me the image, I can't help but be thankful for it.

It's my mom.

She's here with me. She's smiling at me with the beautiful toothy smile that I've missed so much. Her hair is combed straight, parted down the middle, and resting off to either side, framing her face. She doesn't speak, but I can *feel* what she wants me to know.

None of this is my doing. I didn't hurt that homeowner. I didn't make Evan break into my house. And I didn't chase him into the street.

I want to keep my eyes closed in this moment and stay with my mom forever. I don't want to have to say goodbye. Not again.

Her smile stretches wider. Her look

assures me that I can revisit this version of her whenever I want, but that it is important for me to not take ownership of what's happened these last few days. I can regret it, but I don't need to blame myself for it.

And I don't have to forgive myself because there is nothing to be forgiven.

I open my eyes.

Evan is gone.

15

We take a break from cleaning up the house to enjoy some hot chocolate.

Madelyn gets the water boiling while I pull a trio of mugs from the cupboard. I spot a nail sticking out from beneath the kitchen cabinets and snatch it up, tossing it into the bucket with the others.

"I got the doorknob switched back," Liam says as he steps into the kitchen with a screwdriver in his hand. He drops it into the toolbox and then removes the pair of gloves that made it possible for him to touch the iron doorknob.

The clang of metal on metal causes me to flinch. I'm guessing it will take me a few days to build my nerves back up and rediscover some semblance of normalcy. Let's be honest, maybe a few weeks.

"I don't know why you don't just keep the iron one on the door. It looks way better," he adds.

I line the mugs up in a row along the counter. "You're just saying that so I'll always have to hold the door open for you. Plus, how do you expect me to explain that to my dad? 'Oh, I got bored and thought I'd do a few renovations on the place while you were out tracking down a zombie that I summoned'?"

Liam plops his body down onto one of the chairs at the kitchen table. "Well, when you put it that way, it doesn't sound worth it."

I scoff as I pour the packets of instant hot chocolate into the mugs.

Madelyn comes in behind me and empties the boiling water into each of them. Steam rises from out of the tea kettle as she places it back onto the stove.

I deliver the three mugs to the table, placing one in front of Liam. He takes it in his hand and chugs its contents down in one gulp, not at all affected by the scalding hot liquid running down his throat. Where he's from in The Pit, heat takes on an entirely different meaning.

"So . . ." I say, not really knowing where to take the conversation.

Madelyn sees this as an opportunity to offer up her own theory to the rest of us.

"I think I have a pretty good idea of what happened," she says, sitting down at the table. She wraps her hands around the mug of hot chocolate and uses it to warm up her hands. "You let Boo-en in. You let him possess you. The residual demonic energy that he left behind fueled your subconscious and gave it a supernatural jump start. You blamed yourself and felt like you needed to be held accountable, so you took control of Evan. That served to both give him his life back but also to punish yourself."

I sip from my hot chocolate, thinking about Madelyn's theory. It makes as much sense as anything could in this situation. "But where is he now? Evan, I mean?"

Madelyn shrugs. "I don't know. Considering your dad is still out looking for him, we know he didn't return to the morgue. I asked Boo-en to see if he could find out anything for us. There's a chance that Evan ended up in The Pit."

"No way," Liam says, sliding his empty mug across the table. "He wasn't a demon, so he wouldn't wind up in The Pit." Liam pauses. "I actually have my own theory, if anyone would care to hear it?"

Both Madelyn and I glance across the table at Liam. He looks proud of himself for having come up with an idea that the rest of us want to hear.

"I think he's inside you, Damon."

I practically do a spit take with my hot chocolate when I hear Liam's theory out loud.

"What?" I ask.

Liam sways back and forth in his chair. "It was your emotions that brought him back, right? Well, what if Evan just went back inside you where he's, you know, locked away?"

"So basically, he's like a repressed emotion?" Madelyn asks.

Liam shrugs.

I glance over at Madelyn. She considers Liam's theory and doesn't immediately discredit it. This worries me.

"Great!" I announce, standing up from the table. "Now I have someone else's tortured soul living inside of me?"

Madelyn continues to sip from her hot chocolate. She is the best of us when it comes to thinking rationally, but there isn't anything rational about what we've experienced these last twenty-four hours.

"It's possible," she says. "But then again, anything is. We'll keep looking into it until we narrow the possibilities down. In the meantime, we should get back to cleaning this place up. Your dad will give up his search eventually. We still have a lot to do."

Liam's finger shoots up to his face, and he uses it to touch the tip of his nose. "I call not cleaning up the salt downstairs!"

I give in and head off toward the basement stairs. "It's fine. I've got it. You vacuum all of the Boo-en flakes off of the couch. But when you're done, don't you dare lie down and take a nap. If you do, I'm pouring this salt all over you."

"Hey, pal," Liam says jokingly, "easy with your emotions. We don't need you setting off another doomsday event every time you get upset."

I look down at the floor. There is a nail caught under the lip of the stairs. I fish it out with my foot and then kick it across the tiles in Liam's direction. It slams into his big toe and causes a tiny burst of flames to appear on it. He yelps and jumps up and down, stamping the fire out.

"Not cool!" he shouts.

Madelyn and I laugh as we go off to do our individual chores.

As I reach the bottom of the basement stairs, I pause and close my eyes. Madelyn and Liam are both upstairs, so I'm by myself. At least for the moment.

She doesn't appear right away. In fact, I'm frustrated by the delay, but I know I'm to blame. It's because I'm having a difficult time keeping my thoughts straight.

But when I focus—really focus—I see her smile appear somewhere deep within the darkness. Each tooth glistens like a little beacon of hope.

Mom.

ABOUT THE AUTHOR

When not writing in his spiral notebooks, Jason M. Burns can be found outside getting his tattoo-covered arms dirty where he spends the warmer months hybridizing daylilies and tending to his koi pond. Type A even when typing, he has written and created a number of critically-acclaimed and commercially successful comic book series and graphic novels, including *Magical Pet Vet* and *Jericho: Season 3*, which appeared on the *New York Times* Best Sellers list. He has spearheaded book lines for *Sesame Street* and the DreamWorks Animation stable of titles and most recently served as Chief Creative Officer for Neymar Jr. Comics, the publishing company of international soccer star Neymar Jr. There his writing was translated across six languages and reached over forty million people worldwide. In addition to comic books, Burns also works in Hollywood where he has a number of television and film projects in development. He is also co-host of the popular podcast series *What About*, which he produces alongside actor Danny Nucci (*Titanic*, *The Fosters*).

Burns lives in Massachusetts with his wife, two children, and a trio of rescue dogs with unnecessarily silly names, Bark W. Grizwold, Maisy Gray, and Bad Bad Leroy Brown.